Adapted by Alice Alfonsi
Based on the series created by
Michael Poryes
Susan Sherman
Part One is based on the teleplay written
by Bob Keyes & Doug Keyes.
Part Two is based on the teleplay written
by Chip Keyes.

VOLO

New York

Printed in the United States of America

First Edition
1 3 5 7 9 10 8 6 4 2

Library of Congress Control Number on file.

ISBN 0-7868-4658-5

For more Disney Press fun, visit www.disneybooks.com
Visit DisneyChannel.com

that's SO
raven

Part One

Chapter One

Raven Baxter glanced around the empty gymnasium.

"Eddie?" she called, tapping her stacked black boot against the slick wood floor. *"Hello?"*

With a frown, Raven checked her watch. Her best friend, Eddie Thomas, had asked her to meet him here during lunch period. Well, here she was. So, where was he?

A minute later, the lights dimmed. A spotlight came on. Static crackled over the loudspeakers, and a voice echoed off the gymnasium's brick walls.

". . . And now, introducing the newest member of Bayside's basketball team: Starting Guard Eddie 'Nothin-But-Net' Thomas!"

The lights came up, and Eddie burst through the locker room doors. "Three seconds left," he called, dribbling across the court. "Thomas charges down the floor. He makes his move, drops to the rim—" *Swish!* The ball greased through the net like it was covered in butter. "Yes! Thomas wins the championship!" cried Eddie. "And the crowd goes wild!"

Not just the crowd, Raven thought with a grin. Eddie had been practicing for months to make the cut. Now he'd done it—he'd made his dream come true. "Congratulations, Eddie!" she squealed, her heels clicking across the gym floor. "You made the team! I'm so happy for you!"

"Thank you, thank you," said Eddie as Raven threw her arms around him. Smiling, he waited for his best friend to end her Big Squeeze.

It was a *long* wait.

Okay, thought Eddie, there's such a thing as feeling the love *too* much. "Uh, and now the crowd can *stop* hugging," he told her.

"That's right," said Raven, realizing she was doing the *girly* thing. Which was not cool, because Eddie was a *guy* friend.

Think *macho*, Raven told herself. "Woof, woof, woof!" she shouted in a deep voice, her fist pumping the air. "Home doggie, awright. High five!" Then she slapped Eddie's hand and asked, "So, when did you find out?"

"This morning." Eddie twirled the ball on his finger. "Coach says I'm starting guard for the rest of the season. I just have to pull at least a C-plus on all my midterms."

"Oh," said Raven.

"Right on," said Eddie.

He tossed the basketball to Raven. But when she held out her hands, she caught more than just the ball. She also snagged a glimpse of the future. . . .

Through her eye
The vision runs
Flash of future
Here it comes—

I see the top of a desk.

Now I see a hand. It's holding a piece of paper. Uh-oh, it's a test paper. Spanish class. Multiple choice.

Whoa! Looks like a packet of ketchup exploded on the page. Every single question has an angry red circle around the correct answer, which means the kid who took this test got almost every question wrong.

Now I'm seeing the name on top of the test. . . .

Oh, no. No, no, no—the name I'm seeing cannot be Eddie Thomas.

But it is . . . and now I'm seeing Eddie's face. He's looking at his grade—a big fat letter in a big red circle.

"An F?" he cries. He looks totally crushed!

When the vision ended, Raven blinked—and saw Eddie staring at her.

"What? What? What? Did you have a vision?" he asked. "Did it have anything to do with me dating a cheerleader . . . and *another* cheerleader?"

"Eddie," said Raven. "I have visions, not fantasies."

Eddie raised an eyebrow. Okay, he thought, so the cheerleader scenario was out. But he still wanted to know what Raven had seen.

Raven blinked at Eddie then swallowed nervously. "But you know," she said, chickening out, "it wasn't anything important."

Eddie sighed with relief. Then he took

back the basketball and threw it in a perfect arc across the court. *Whoosh!* The ball sailed through the hoop.

"Man," Eddie said with a grin, "this is the best day of my life. Nothing can stop me now."

Nothing but a big red F on your next Spanish test, thought Raven. But she didn't dare tell him. How could she?

"Yeah, right," Raven said. "Nothing."

Chapter Two

"**S**o, if Eddie gets an F on his test," said Raven, pacing back and forth in the girls' bathroom, "he'll get kicked off the team."

Raven's other best friend, Chelsea Daniels, stood at the bathroom mirror, sawing at her teeth with a yard of dental floss—her usual post-lunch ritual.

"Ya utta ell im," Chelsea garbled as she earnestly polished each tooth.

"I know, I've gotta tell him," Raven replied. She had long ago learned how to translate Chelsea floss-speak. "But he was so psyched about being on the team, I just don't know how."

"An u ee ure ih aas eheee's est?" asked Chelsea.

"Yes, I'm sure it was Eddie's test!" cried Raven. "He was holding it in his hand. And the right answers were circled, like D, A, B, A . . . I remember it spelled out DABA, B-B, CABA, C-C, BAD, DAD, D-D, CABA—"

Chelsea took the floss out of her mouth. "Raven!" she shrieked.

Raven's eyes suddenly widened. "I know!" she cried in realization. "I have the answers to Eddie's test."

"No," said Chelsea. "You said 'Dee Dee.' That's my aunt's name!"

Raven sighed. This girl is obviously flossing the wrong part of her head, she thought. Maybe she should try between her *ears*.

"Do you know what this means, Chelsea?" said Raven, making it plain. "I could give the answers to Eddie. He'll get an A on his Spanish midterm. And then he won't get kicked off the team."

"You're right," said Chelsea. "You should tell him."

"Yeah . . ." Raven wanted to. She really did. "But that would be cheating, and I can't do that," she said.

"You're right," agreed Chelsea. "There's no way you can tell him."

"No," said Raven, "but if I don't, he'll get kicked off the team."

Chelsea's forehead furrowed in confusion. "Then you should tell him," she said.

"Oh, so you believe in *cheating*?" asked Raven.

"What do you want from me?" cried Chelsea.

"I want *you* to be the one who's psychic," said Raven in frustration, "so I could be the one saying, 'What are you gonna do?'"

Chelsea scratched her head and thought. No doubt about it, this was a tough one. Should Raven help Eddie cheat? Or should she keep her lips zipped and watch her best friend's big dream get crushed? Chelsea figured there really was only one way to reply. "So," she said, "what are you gonna do?"

Raven just shook her head. Why do I even bother? she wondered.

"Okay, Max," Eddie told his new teammate later that afternoon, "we're going to need some nicknames now that we're on the team. Like 'The Mailman' or 'Shaq.'"

Max nodded as he and Eddie walked down the crowded hallway. "Okay," he said, "um, I'll be Shaq."

Eddie stared at Max. He could not believe he'd found the one kid in America who'd never heard of Shaquille O'Neal.

Max noticed Eddie looking at him. "Don't tell me it's already taken?" he said.

"Eddie," called Raven, rushing up the hall

with Chelsea right behind her. "Don't you have a Spanish midterm tomorrow?"

"Yeah," said Eddie.

"So, uh, how are you doing in that class?" she asked, trying to sound casual.

"Okay," Eddie said with a shrug. "I mean, I'll probably pull off a C."

He turned and walked over to his locker. Raven was right on his heels.

"Okay, Eddie, listen—" Raven began, but she stopped when she realized Max was still standing there. "Hey, Max," Raven said, "can we get a minute?"

Max grinned. "Uh, sure."

But instead of giving her some privacy with Eddie, Max threw his arm around Raven's shoulders and steered her to the other side of the hall.

"So, uh, what did you want to talk to me about?" he asked.

"Well, you know," said Raven, "I just wanted to talk to *Eddie* alone. Really."

"Well, he's right over there," said Max. "What are you talking to *me* for?"

Dang, thought Raven, this kid needs to visit Lost and Found, 'cause he's clearly missing some brain cells!

With a forced smile, she told Max, "I guess I wasn't thinking."

Max nodded. "I have those days sometimes."

"I bet you do," said Raven, patting Max's cheek.

As Max strode down the hall, Raven rushed back to her best friend. "Eddie, listen," she said, "you really have to concentrate on those grades. You know, you've got to keep them up."

"I know, I know," said Eddie. "Look, I'll study tonight. I'm meeting the guys over at Max's house to watch the game."

Seeing Raven's worried look, Chelsea stepped up to the plate. "Hey," she said brightly, "why go out and have fun with the guys when you can come over to Raven's for a *study party*?"

"Now, that is cool," agreed Raven.

"Yeah!" exclaimed Chelsea.

"And then maybe afterwards," said Eddie, batting his eyelashes, "we can sit around, do each other's toenails, and share our *feelings*?"

"Yeah!" said Chelsea.

"No!" cried Eddie. How could these two be so dense? he wondered. Like he'd *ever* choose a "study party" over a night watching b-ball with his new teammates? "I mean, it's not like you had a vision of me failing the test or something," he told Raven, turning to go. But when he saw the look Raven gave Chelsea, he stopped dead in his tracks. "Did you?" he asked in a choked voice.

"Sorry, Eddie," said Raven softly.

"Oh, man!" Eddie exploded. "I can't get an F on this test. I'll get kicked off the team!"

"Hey, Eddie, don't panic, okay?" said Chelsea. "You always cram the night before and get a good grade. Which, by the way, is so irritating. Do you know how hard it is—"

"Chelsea!" Raven interrupted, halting what she knew was about to become a typical runaway train of thought. "Focus."

"I can cram all I want to, y'all," Eddie told them. "I just don't get Spanish."

"You know what, Eddie?" said Raven. "We are not going to let this vision come true. You know why? 'Cause we both took Spanish last year. And you know, not to brag, but we both did—"

Raven and Chelsea improvised a few flamenco steps. *Excellente!* they shouted in unison.

"Huh?" asked Eddie.

"That's *excellent* in Spanish," Raven explained.

Eddie threw up his hands. "Then why don't they just say that?" he asked.

¡Ay caramba! thought Raven. We've got our work cut out for us.

Chapter Three

At Raven's house later that evening, Raven and Chelsea tried tutoring Eddie the old fashioned way—by cracking the books. But Eddie just wasn't getting it. So, the girls came up with a new way of teaching him.

"All right, contestant!" announced Raven, sitting on a stool in the kitchen. "Are you ready to play another round of 'Do You Want to Pass Spanish?'"

"Yes, I am, Raven," Eddie said agreeably. He'd do anything—*anything*—to make sure he stayed on the basketball team.

"All right," said Raven, "in the last round, you managed to correctly label, in Spanish, an amount of *zero* items." She frowned. "You can stop now or you could push on to actually *learn* something!"

"I'd like to learn something," said Eddie, nodding like a bobblehead doll.

"All right. Chelsea," said Raven, "let's tell Eddie and the folks at home what he's playing for."

"All right, Raven!" Chelsea chirped from the kitchen table. "Eddie's playing for an ice-cold root beer." She presented the bottle with a flashy wave and smiled like a game show hostess. "Courtesy of your mom and dad. Yes! Your mom and dad—makers of you and Cory."

"All right," said Raven, checking her watch. "Ready . . . set . . . go!"

As the seconds ticked by, Eddie rushed around the kitchen, slapping Spanish flash cards on various objects. When his time was up, Eddie gasped for breath. But he was also smiling. "You're right," he told Raven. "This is a cool way to learn Spanish."

Raven glanced around the room and sighed. "All right, Chelsea," she said, "let's tell him how he did."

"Well, on the bright side, Eddie," said Chelsea, "you knew that *telefono* meant, you know, telephone." She reached over to the phone and flipped the card around to reveal the English word written on the back.

Thrilled that he *finally* got an answer right, Eddie began to dance around the room. "Go Eddie, it's your birthday. It's your birthday—"

"Oh, contestant," Raven interrupted sweetly, "but that's where your luck *ran out*." She walked over to the stove and flipped the flash card Eddie had placed there. "Because, you see, we don't cook—in the *garbage*."

"*Eehhh!*" Chelsea made a noise like a game show "loser" buzzer.

Next, Raven walked over to a kitchen chair. "And we don't sit—" she told Eddie, flipping another flash card—"on a *shoe*."

"*Eehhh!*" cried Chelsea again.

"But if you're sitting on that shoe," said Raven, walking toward a carton of milk on the counter, "you can have an ice cold drink of—" she flipped the card—"*tuna.*"

"*Eehhh!*" cried Chelsea one more time.

"Will you stop doing that?" Eddie barked.

Chelsea was about to point out that she was simply adding the appropriate sound effect to inspire and motivate Eddie—when Raven's little brother Cory strode into the room, interrupting them.

"Dad says these guys have to go," Cory told Raven. "It's getting late."

Raven frowned. "Can you please tell him another fifteen minutes? Eddie's got a really important Spanish test tomorrow."

"Spanish?" Cory exclaimed. He turned to Eddie. "*That's* why you've been here all night?"

Eddie nodded. Cory threw up his hands and cried, "*¡Ay caramba! Solo tengo dies años y yo puedo hablar Español. Eres estupido y me desagradas. ¿Que clase de hombre eres?*" Then he turned in a huff and headed for the door, adding, "*¡Estupido! Estupido!*"

Raven understood that Cory had bragged that he was only ten and *he* could speak Spanish. And he'd thrown in a few insults for good measure. For once, Raven was glad that Eddie couldn't speak Spanish. Otherwise, her little brother might have found himself headed for Spain—minus the "S."

"There's no way I'm gonna get this stuff by tomorrow," Eddie told Raven and Chelsea with a sigh. "I mean, maybe if I had a couple more days, I could just . . ."

"Eddie, don't give up, okay?" Raven said

with determination. "Because we're not. Now, I want you to go to the living room so we can make up some more cards."

His head hanging, Eddie trudged out of the kitchen.

"What are we going to do, Chelsea?" Raven asked quietly. "He's not getting it."

"I know," said Chelsea. "Maybe you should just tell him you saw—"

Seeing Eddie pop back into the room for his Spanish textbook, Raven tried to cut Chelsea off. "Hold it!" she cried. "Uh, I *saw* the Big Dipper and, you know, the lunar eclipse."

"No, no, no," said Chelsea. She hadn't noticed that Eddie had come back. "I meant, tell him that you saw the *answers.*"

Eddie's jaw dropped. "You saw the answers, Rae?" he cried excitedly.

"Yeah," Raven admitted unhappily. "That was, uh, the part of my vision I left out."

"This is great!" cried Eddie. "So where are they? You got 'em written down or what?"

It pained Raven, but she had to say it. "Eddie, that would be cheating. And I just can't help you do that."

"I know," said Eddie. "But can't you think of it as . . . 'psychic tutoring'?"

"I'm sorry," said Raven as gently as she could. "I just can't."

"Wait a minute," said Eddie, unable to believe his ears. "You mean to tell me that you're just going to let me fail and get kicked off the team? You know how many guys tried out, Rae? And I made the cut. That makes me *something* around here."

"I know, Eddie," said Raven, "but—"

"Just forget it," said Eddie, storming toward the door.

"You know, it's not that easy for me, either,"

Raven tried to tell him. But Eddie wasn't hearing it.

"Poor Raven," he snapped sarcastically. "It must be *so* hard knowing stuff before it happens." The hurt look on Eddie's face made Raven want to cry. "I thought you were my friend," he told her.

"I am," she assured him.

But this time it was Eddie's turn to sound the "loser" buzzer.

"*Eehhh!*" he said. "That's the *wrong* answer."

Chapter Four

The next day at school, Raven brightened when she saw Eddie walking down the hallway.

"Hey, Eddie," she said cheerfully.

But Eddie walked right by her without a word.

Hurt, Raven turned to Chelsea. "Can you believe him?" she said. "I wish I never had that stupid vision."

"There's nothing you can do now, Rae," said Chelsea. "His test is in an hour."

Just then, Eddie's Spanish teacher strolled by, saying hello to her students.

"*Hola*, Ricardo! *Hola*, Miguel!" called Señorita Rodriguez. "I hope you're ready for the big test today. I am. But then again, *I* know the answers."

You and me both, Raven thought with a sigh. If only Eddie had a few more days to study . . .

Suddenly, Raven turned to Chelsea and said, "Maybe there *is* something I can do."

Raven headed straight for Señorita Rodriguez's classroom. She found the Spanish teacher standing at the back, looking out the tall windows. Outside, two window washers in bright yellow coveralls stood on a hanging scaffold.

"Eh, eh, eh," the teacher called out to one of them. "You missed a spot."

The man on the scaffold put a hand to his ear. He'd obviously had trouble hearing the teacher through the thick glass.

"You missed a spot!" the teacher called louder.

The window washer rubbed at the spot on the glass where Señorita Rodriguez was pointing.

"Still there," the teacher told him.

The man rubbed a little more.

"Still there," the teacher repeated.

Frowning in frustration, the window washer rubbed *a lot* more.

"Okay, all gone!" cried Señorita Rodriguez, finally satisfied.

Whoa, thought Raven, I forgot how hard this *señorita* was to please! Swallowing hard, Raven stepped forward. "Señorita Rodriguez, hi," she said.

"Raven," said the Spanish teacher.

"You got a minute?" asked Raven.

"I haven't seen you all year," said the teacher. Suddenly, Señorita Rodriguez's eyes narrowed. "You have a little something, right here," she told Raven, pointing to her teeth.

With the side of one finger, Raven rubbed her front teeth.

"Still there," insisted the teacher.

Raven rubbed a little more.

"Still there," the teacher repeated.

Dang, thought Raven, rubbing one more time, where's Chelsea and her dental floss when you need her?

"Okay, all gone," said the teacher, finally satisfied.

Raven could see this wasn't going to be easy. But she'd come this far, so she figured she might as well go for the whole enchilada.

"I have something really important I need to tell you," said Raven. She made a show of glancing over her shoulder and lowering her voice. "Some of your students are worried about how hard the midterm test is going to be today."

"What can I tell you?" said Señorita Rodriguez with a dismissive wave. "Spanish is not for sissies."

"Don't I know it. But it's just that some of them are thinking that they may just switch to—" Raven paused for dramatic effect. "French."

"What?" Señorita Rodriguez cried. "I bet that new French teacher, Madame What's-Her-Face, is behind this. I don't trust that woman. She's about as French as french fries. And yet she prances around with her croissants and her international coffee like she's all that!" In a huff, the Spanish teacher snapped her fingers this way and that—the universal sign for "she's all that."

Raven had to swallow a smile. She couldn't believe her plan was actually working.

"I'm just saying," continued Raven, "that I think you need to give your students a little bit more time to study. You know, you could always postpone the test until Monday—"

Raven held her breath and watched the teacher mull this over.

"Postpone the test? Hmm," said Señorita Rodriguez, considering the request.

"So, you'll do it?" Raven asked hopefully.

"No," said the teacher.

Raven's shoulders sank.

"They'll just have to do the best they can," said the teacher. Then she turned her attention to the papers on her desk. "*Adios*, Raven."

As she turned to go, Raven absently noticed one of the window washers working diligently.

"Señorita," she called to the teacher, "you can tell him he's going to have to do *that* one again."

The teacher looked in confusion at the sparkling glass. But before she could ask what in the world Raven was talking about, a gull flew by and a big white splat hit the window. Raven wasn't surprised. In her experience, seeing the future was a messy business.

Chapter Five

Down on the first floor, Eddie stood by his locker, talking with his new teammate, Max.

"I'd better get to class," Max said, glancing at his watch. "But don't forget, team pictures on Monday."

"At least I'll have something to prove I was on the team," Eddie said, angrily trying to push his basketball into his locker. But the locker was too narrow. "Dang," he mumbled. "Stupid ball."

"Wait, wait, wait." Max took the basketball from Eddie. "Turn it on its *side*," Max instructed in a knowing tone. Then he rotated the basketball and pushed.

Eddie rolled his eyes, watching Max struggle with the round ball. *Of course* the dang thing still wasn't going to fit, Eddie thought. Was this boy mental?

Max finally stopped pushing. He stared at the basketball, confused. "That's funny," he told Eddie. "It worked for my football."

"Go," Eddie said in frustration, taking the ball back. "Go on, Max. Go."

Eddie's foul mood had officially sunk to off-the-charts nasty. He knew the only thing that could make him feel worse was seeing Raven.

Just then, he heard a familiar voice say, "Um, hey, Eddie. Can we talk?"

"Raven," said Eddie, glaring over his shoulder. "Wait!" He put a hand to his ear. "I thought I heard a *former* friend of mine."

Just then, the bell rang.

"Man, I've got a Spanish test to fail," Eddie told Raven. "Here—" He handed her his basketball. "You might as well take this. I won't be needing it."

Raven looked down at Eddie's beloved b-ball. When she looked up again, she saw her best friend trudging toward the staircase that would take him to his midterm test, his failing grade, and the big end to his big dream. Raven hated the idea of cheating—or helping anyone cheat. But Eddie had been a true friend to her for a long time. He had never let her down. And she couldn't let him down now. She just couldn't.

"Eddie, wait," called Raven.

Eddie stopped and turned.

"I'll give you the answers," Raven said with a sigh.

"You will?" Eddie's face lit up like a scoreboard. He rushed to Raven and wrapped his arms around her. "Oh, I knew you'd come through for me!" he cried. "What are they?"

"They're D, A, B, A, C-C," she began to rattle off.

"*Whoa!* Slow down, slow down," said Eddie. "D, A, B, what?"

Raven exchanged Eddie's basketball for his notebook, turned to a blank page, and took out a pen.

"I'll write them down for you," she told him.

Eddie grinned. "Man, you got my back on this one, Rae. I mean, if you *ever* need anything, like a kidney, I will personally—" He paused. Test answers were one thing, thought Eddie, but major body organs? Naw, he wasn't going there. "I will personally *find* someone to *donate* it to you," he finished.

Then he grabbed his notebook from Raven and vaulted up the stairs, memorizing the answers as he ran.

"Good lookin' out, Rae," he called over his shoulder.

Raven glanced at Chelsea, who'd been watching the whole scene from across the hall. "Well," said Raven, "at least *he's* happy."

"He didn't give you much of a choice, Rae," said Chelsea.

Just then, the girls noticed Eddie's Spanish teacher walking toward them, carrying an armload of pink papers.

"*Hola*, Chelsea. *Hola*, Raven," said Señorita Rodriguez. She turned to Raven. "I thought about what you said about students switching to French," she said. "I can't let that happen."

"So you're postponing the test?" Raven asked hopefully.

"No," said Señorita Rodriguez. "I decided to make Spanish more fun. So I made a whole *new* test. With *all new* questions."

"Is it any easier?" asked Chelsea.

"No," said Señorita Rodriguez. "But I

printed it on pink paper—and that says *fun* to me! *Adios.*"

A new test with all new questions meant one thing, Raven realized—*new answers*! She exchanged a glance with Chelsea, then the two girls dashed for the stairs. They had to warn Eddie!

Señorita Rodriguez walked briskly through the aisles of her packed classroom, placing a copy of the Spanish midterm facedown on every student's desk.

"I got a D, I got an A, I got a B-A-D-D," Eddie rapped to himself as he sat there waiting for the test to start. In fact, he was so concerned with trying to keep all the multiple-choice answers straight in his head, he barely noticed Raven as she burst through the classroom door.

"Hey, Ms. Señorita," called Raven, "I have a

message from the office for Mr. Eddie Thomas."

"Raven," the teacher said disapprovingly, "he's about to take a test."

"I understand that," said Raven, edging across the room, "but it's really important. Here, I'll let you in on a little secret. His uncle Louie is in the hospital. And see, what happened was he got the *wrong test*—"

By now, Raven had reached Eddie's desk. "So what happened," she continued, "is they gave him the completely *wrong test*. Do you understand that, Eddie? Your Uncle Louie has completely the *wrong test. Comprendé?*"

But Eddie just stared at Raven in confusion. "I don't have an Uncle Louie," he told her.

Señorita Rodriguez threw up her hands. "It must be a mistake, okay," she said, ushering Raven out. "Now if you'll excuse us—"

"A mistake?" Raven repeated desperately as

the teacher pushed her toward the door. "Then I must have the *wrong information*." Raven practically shouted the words back at Eddie. "It's funny how people can get mixed up and get the *wrong information*. I think you need to tell him, you know, he got the *wrong information*."

"Raven," said the teacher when they finally reached the doorway, "Eduardo obviously doesn't care about his uncle, so—bye-bye!"

Before Raven knew it, she'd been tossed out. The classroom door shut behind her.

But Raven wasn't giving up that easily. Together Raven and Chelsea made a hand-written sign that read, NEW TEST—WRONG ANSWERS! They waved it in front of the small window in the classroom door. But before they could get Eddie to look their way, Señorita Rodriguez pulled down the door's window shade.

"All right, class," the teacher announced, walking to her big, wooden desk at the back of the room. "Start your tests. You have until the end of my Ricky Martin CD." The teacher happily put on her headphones. "And *go*."

As the students turned over their papers and grumbled, Eddie cheerfully took out his pencil and began to quietly rap to himself—

"I got a D, I got an A, I got a B-A-D-D . . . I got a C, I got an A, I got a B-D-D." Eddie grinned. "And I *most definitely* don't got no F!"

Chapter Six

"**R**emind me again why we're risking detention?" asked Chelsea.

"Girl," said Raven, "we are not going to get detention. I mean, if we get caught up here, we're talking *expelled*."

Up here, as it turned out, was high above the sidewalk, right outside the window of Eddie's Spanish classroom. Raven had convinced Chelsea to join her in putting on a pair of bright yellow coveralls, borrowing the window washer's scaffolding platform, and then lowering the platform from the roof. According to Raven's plan, all they had to do now was get Eddie's attention, show him the NEW TEST—WRONG ANSWERS! sign they'd made, then pull themselves back to the rooftop.

Piece of cake, Raven figured. But, as the platform swayed in the wind, Raven began to realize that piece of cake might be more of the pancake variety—as in *flat.*

No, no, no, she told herself, shutting her eyes. *Don't even go there.*

"Don't worry, Chelsea," said Raven, opening her eyes again. "All we have to do is get Eddie to see the sign, and we'll be all right. Where is it?"

"I taped it to the railing like you told me," said Chelsea.

Raven looked at the railing. Instead of taping the NEW TEST—WRONG ANSWERS! sign to the *classroom* side of the platform, Chelsea had taped it to the *street* side.

"Oh, perfect, Chelsea," said Raven. "Now all we have to do is get Eddie to the other side of the street so he can read the sign."

Suddenly, Raven heard a fluttering sound above her. Something landed lightly on her head.

"Ah, Chelsea?" said Raven, freezing. "Tell me there is *not* a bird on my head."

"Okay, don't move. Don't scare it," said Chelsea. "Because you know what pigeons do when they're scared."

Raven suddenly remembered that white splat the bird had left for the window washers earlier that day. Her eyes opened wide. "Get it off my head," Raven groaned.

"Hey, bird. Shoo, bird," Chelsea said sweetly. But the pigeon didn't move a feather.

"Fly away, little bird. Fly away, little birdie," Chelsea said, even more sweetly.

Nothing.

Finally, Chelsea waved her arms—and the bird took off.

"Hey, look," said Raven, peering into the classroom. "There's Eddie!"

Without thinking, Raven rushed to Chelsea's side of the scaffolding platform, making it sway back and forth. "Okay, Chelsea," said Raven, clutching the rocking platform, "now pay attention. I think we're going to have to go *lower*."

Chelsea nodded and released her side of the rope. Instantly, Chelsea's end of the platform dropped three feet.

"Chelsea!" cried Raven, watching her friend tumble down the steeply tilting platform.

Raven hung on to the railing for dear life. Just then, a big red bucket rolled down the platform and landed right on Chelsea's head.

Belly-down on the platform, Chelsea knocked the bucket off her head and gasped for air.

"Are you okay? Are you okay?" cried Raven, still clinging to the railing. "You're okay?"

Reaching out, Chelsea tugged hard on the rope to get the platform straight again. But the pulley system made the violent tug go twice as far as she'd intended. Now Chelsea's end of the platform tilted steeply up and Raven's end tilted sharply down.

"Ouch! Oww! That's my leg!" cried Raven as Chelsea tumbled over her.

"Go grab the rope. Grab the rope!" Raven commanded.

As Chelsea grabbed the rope to level out the platform, Raven pulled the NEW TEST— WRONG ANSWERS! sign off the railing.

"Okay, I got it," said Raven, relieved. But before she could move it to the other side of the scaffolding rail, a stiff breeze plucked it from her hand. Chelsea lunged for it, but it was too late. The sign was gone with the wind.

Raven wanted to cry. "Do you think maybe Eddie saw just a little bit of it?" she asked pathetically.

Meanwhile, inside the Spanish classroom, Eddie rose from his seat. He'd finished the test before all the other students. Now he was happily walking toward the teacher's desk to turn it in.

"Eddie got up already!" cried Chelsea, peering through the window.

Raven desperately waved, trying to get Eddie's attention. Luckily, the teacher was sitting with her back to the windows and couldn't see a thing.

"You're through early, Eduardo," Señorita Rodriguez said when she noticed him approaching her desk.

"You know, Spanish just comes easy to a brother—" Eddie began to boast. Just then he noticed something freaky going on outside the classroom windows. What the . . . ? he thought.

"*Tienes mucha suerte,*" said the teacher.

Eddie blinked, totally lost. "Uh . . ." He tried to think of a good Spanish-sounding comeback. "Salsa," he said.

Señorita Rodriguez gave him a suspicious look and reached out for his test paper. But Eddie quickly pulled it back. He'd finally noticed Raven and Chelsea on the scaffolding outside.

Whatever this is, thought Eddie, it can't be good. "On second thought," he told the teacher, "it never hurts to double-check your work. Would you mind if I opened a window? It's kind of hot in here."

"Go ahead," said Señorita Rodriguez.

Eddie moved to the far window, opened it, and stuck his head out. "What are y'all doing?" he called softly.

Raven and Chelsea tried to answer him, but it wasn't easy. The scaffolding platform was swinging in the wind. Back and forth it went, like a clock pendulum. The only way the girls could communicate with Eddie was in bits and pieces as they swung past his window.

"You've got—" called Raven, swinging one way—"the wrong answers," she finished, swinging the other.

"Your teacher—" called Chelsea, swinging to the right—"she changed the test!" she added, swinging to the left.

"What?" asked Eddie.

"Don't make us—" called Raven.

"—say it again," finished Chelsea.

"What do I do?" asked Eddie. "I don't know this stuff."

"Just do—" said Raven.

"—the best—" said Chelsea.

"—you can," finished Raven.

From inside the classroom, Señorita Rodriguez called, "Eduardo! *Cierre la ventana!*"

Frowning, Eddie whispered to Raven and Chelsea, "What did she say?"

"Close the window!" replied Chelsea, swinging by one last time.

Eddie did as his teacher asked, then turned and went back to his seat.

"Okay, Chelsea," said Raven. She was about to tell her to even out her side of the platform, when she felt the scaffolding move all by itself.

"Rae, we're leveling out," said Chelsea, amazed. "What are you doing?"

"I'm not doing anything, Chelsea," said Raven.

Together the girls looked up—and gulped.

"The principal is," observed Raven.

Chelsea gave a little wave to the man staring angrily down from the roof. "Hi, Principal Perkins," she called sweetly.

"We'll be right up, okay?" said Raven, as the platform lifted them higher. Yeah, she thought, our own little express elevator—straight to the principal's office.

Chapter Seven

After school that day, Raven found Eddie in the gym shooting baskets alone.

"Hey," she said tentatively. "So, how'd your test go?"

"I don't know," Eddie said with a frown. "The whole thing was kind of a blur. How'd your meeting with the principal go?"

"Oh, yeah. That was kind of a blur, too. A really *loud, angry* blur." Raven shuddered at the memory. She was glad she could put it all behind her—except for the detention, of course.

Eddie shook his head guiltily. "You wouldn't even be in this mess if I didn't ask you to help me cheat. I'm sorry, Rae. And all that stuff I said about you being a bad friend? Well, that was out of line."

"That's okay," said Raven. But she knew it wasn't totally okay. Not yet. In her kitchen the night before, Eddie had said that being on the team had finally made him "*something* around here." Raven had to tell him what she really thought about that.

"I know being on the basketball team means a lot to you," she began. "But you know, you've got a lot more going for you than just that."

Eddie walked off the court and sat down on a wooden bench. "Yeah, right," he said skeptically.

Raven sat down next to him. "Yeah, right," she said sincerely. "I mean, you're the best rapper I know."

"Well, you're not lying there. I am pretty tight," Eddie said with a little smile.

"And funny," said Raven. "You always crack

me up. And generous. I mean, you always split your lunch with me when I forget mine."

"No, actually, Raven, that's Chelsea," said Eddie.

Whoops, thought Raven. "Well, I know one thing for sure," she told him. "If I was in that Spanish class, *you'd* be the one outside that window helping *me.*"

"Me? No way," said Eddie in a teasing tone. But then he nodded and admitted, "In a second."

Raven smiled—and so did Eddie.

"You know, that psychic thing you got going on," said Eddie, "I always thought it would be kind of fun, but it must be pretty tough to deal with sometimes, huh?"

"Sometimes," said Raven. Especially when it almost ruins one of your best friendships, she added silently. But she didn't want to dwell on the bad stuff. Instead she stood up and pointed to Eddie's basketball. "Hey, you want to play some one-on-one?" she asked.

"Girl, I'll wipe the floor with you," bragged Eddie. "You better sit back down."

"Oh, but you haven't seen my moves," Raven shot back. "Don't make me play."

"Bring it on, little missy," challenged Eddie. He tossed the ball to her. "What's up?"

Raven began to dribble around the court. She made a move toward the basket. But Eddie wasn't Bayside's new starting guard for nothing. She could not get around him!

"Wait! Hold up!" Raven cried, suddenly grabbing her knee. "Ow-ow-ow!"

"What's going on?" Eddie asked, concerned. "Are you okay?"

With Eddie *off* guard, Raven quickly drove all the way up to the basket and sank the ball through the hoop.

"Whoo! That was my move!" she informed Eddie. She gave a high kick. "I'm a cheerleader!"

Dang, thought Eddie, shaking his head. He hated to admit it, but he'd been punked by his own best friend!

Eddie held up his hand, and Raven happily slapped him five.

The following Monday morning, Raven and Chelsea waited nervously by Eddie's locker.

When Raven saw Eddie walking down the hall with a pink paper in his hand, she rushed up to him.

"Is that your Spanish test?" she asked. "How'd you do?"

Shaking his head sadly, Eddie held out the paper. "See for yourself," he said.

Raven took the test, bracing herself for the worst.

But there was no big red F at the top of the page. "Oh, Eddie!" Raven cried. "I'm so amazed. You got a C!"

"Plus," noted Eddie. "Put your eyes on the *plus*."

"Way to go, Eddie!" Chelsea squealed, patting him on the back.

"Well, you know, I wouldn't have pulled this off without you guys," he admitted. "I mean, I guess all that cramming really paid off."

"Congratulations, Eddie," said Raven sincerely.

"Shoot. It don't matter," he said, suddenly acting cool. "I mean, I don't care if I'm on the team. It's no big deal."

He glanced at Raven. She wasn't buying it—not for a second.

"Just let it out, Eddie," Raven told him.

"Really?" he asked.

Raven nodded. All she'd ever wanted was for

Eddie to be happy—and a second later, he was leaping higher than an NBA center.

"I'm on the team!" he crowed.

Eddie's shout was so loud and so pure, Raven was sure its echo could be heard beyond the walls of Bayside Junior High—

"I'm on the team!"

—beyond San Francisco.

"I'm on the team!"

—beyond even planet Earth.

"I'm on the team!"

Dang, thought Raven. Now if that's not the sound of a dream coming true, I don't know what is!

Part Two

Chapter One

Slammin', thought Raven Baxter. Well, *almost*.

Kneeling in front of her dressmaker's mannequin, Raven surveyed her latest creation. The beaded bustier was ready to wear, but the silk print skirt still had issues. Namely, the waistline. It was way too snug. Raven rose to her feet, patted the dummy's tummy, and sighed.

"Chrissy," she said (because every seamstress should be on a first-name basis with her mannequin), "you're gonna need to spend a few more hours in the gym, sweetie, to tighten that up."

Just then, Raven's ten-year-old brother, Cory, walked through her bedroom door.

"I need to use your bathroom," he declared.

Raven's lips wrinkled like a prune. As far as she was concerned, the attic was her domain. Only under the most dire circumstances would she let her little worm of a brother use her private powder room.

"Um, what's wrong with the one downstairs?" asked Raven.

"Dad just used that one," said Cory.

And *that* was a dire circumstance, Raven thought. "Say no more," she told her brother.

Cory headed for the bathroom. "Mom says if we hurry, she'll drive us to school," he announced.

At the mention of her mother, Raven's head began to spin. Her skin tingled, then the whole world seemed to freeze in time—

**Through her eye
The vision runs
Flash of future
Here it comes—**

I see my mother's face.
Weird. She's hanging upside down.
Now, she's starting to say something—
"Listen, what are you doing Saturday?"

"Cory!" Raven cried, coming out of her trance. "I just had a vision that Mom wants to spend some 'quality time' with one of us this weekend."

"Quality time?" squealed Cory, horrified. "I'm going over to Jeremy's tomorrow. He just got his tonsils out and we're feeding them to his snake. What are you doing?"

Raven mentally reviewed her upcoming social schedule—and came up blank.

"Well, nothing," she confessed.

Cory smiled a smug, little-brother smile that told Raven she was doomed.

"But it's Friday! I mean, I can still get an offer," Raven said hopefully. "Where's Mom now?"

"Waiting for us in the living room," Cory said ominously.

"Then I'm going through the *kitchen*," said Raven. She bolted for the back steps.

"Me, too! I can pee at school!" Cory cried.

They both rushed down the narrow staircase, jostling for first place.

"Get out of my way!" complained Raven as Cory tried to squeeze by her.

"I've gotta get my backpack!" shouted Cory.

Raven raced for the kitchen table, where she'd left her books, and Cory hurried to the counter to retrieve his backpack.

Suddenly, a voice interrupted them.

"Kids?" Mrs. Baxter called from the living room.

Cory and Raven froze. A second later, Raven dived under the kitchen table. Cory tried to climb under with her, but Raven's big boot sent him back into the danger zone. Trapped in the middle of the kitchen, Cory had no place to hide. Just then, their mother entered.

"Have you seen Raven?" Mrs. Baxter asked her son.

"Oh, you want *Raven*," said Cory. He glanced under the kitchen table like a cat eyeing a canary.

Raven gave her brother a desperate look. *Puh-lease* do not give me away, she silently begged. For once in your life, Cory, keep that pie-hole shut!

Cory winked reassuringly at his big sister. Raven exhaled with relief. *Wow*, little bro, you are all right, she thought. For this, I owe you one.

That's when Cory turned to Mrs. Baxter, pointed under the table, and declared, "She's right here."

Yeah, Raven thought with a scowl, I owe Cory one all right—one serious slappin'!

Mrs. Baxter leaned over the edge of the table and peered down at Raven, who stared back at her mother's upside-down face. This was starting to look just like her vision.

"What are you doing under there?" Mrs. Baxter asked.

Raven shrugged innocently. "Mama, can't a girl just chill under her own kitchen table?"

Mrs. Baxter smiled. "Listen," she said, "what are you doing Saturday?"

There it is, thought Raven. "*This* Saturday?" she asked uneasily.

Mrs. Baxter nodded. "Um-hmm. Now, if you have plans that's fine. It's not like I'm going to *guilt* you into it by saying it has been *soooo* long since we did anything together . . . even though it *has*. Now, how about it? Got any plans?"

Raven climbed out from under the table. "No, nothing," she replied honestly. Though some great offer was sure to come up at school today, she thought. So, just in case . . . "But *something* probably—" Raven said, hedging, until her mother's hopeful look guilted her into adding—"with you."

Mrs. Baxter grinned from ear to ear. Cory stomped his foot.

"Oh, man," he told his mother. "And *I* wanted to spend Saturday with you."

What a bogus act, thought Raven, watching the little worm shake his head with mock sadness.

"But I wouldn't want to disappoint Raven," Cory added, taking his sister's hand in his. "Because that's how much I love you."

Before Raven could reach out and wring the maggot's neck, her mother pulled them both into a simultaneous embrace.

Dang, thought Raven, foiled by a group hug.

Chapter Two

Later that day, as Raven and Eddie moved through the crowded school hallway, she couldn't help complaining about her messed-up weekend.

"I love my mom," Raven told Eddie. "Just not on *Saturdays.*"

Suddenly, she stopped. A familiar tingly feeling made her grab Eddie's shoulder. "Freeze," she warned him.

A few feet away, a girl was opening a bottle of cola. The bottle exploded, spraying everyone around her. Only Raven and Eddie stayed dry.

"Love that you're psychic," Eddie told Raven.

"Me, too," Raven said, stroking her sleek maroon jacket. "Soda does *not* go with suede."

"So, what's the big deal about hanging with your mom tomorrow?" asked Eddie.

Raven shrugged. Maybe Eddie was right, she thought. Was she making too big a deal out of the whole thing?

"You know what?" she said. "I guess there's nothing happening this weekend anyway."

Just then, a girl named Denise hurried over to Raven.

"Hey, Raven," she said. "We're going Rollerblading by the beach Saturday. You want to come?"

Do I ever! thought Raven. But before she could reply, more kids showed up.

"Rae!" a girl named Jackie cried excitedly. "I have an extra ticket to the Alicia Keys concert Saturday."

Raven groaned.

"I'm having this pool party Saturday," said a boy named Curtis. "It's a barbecue. You like steak or lobster? I'm inviting the whole class over for karaoke!"

Raven groaned even louder.

"And we're going water-skiing, too," Denise continued. "We can check out the lifeguards! It's gonna be *sooo* cool."

"The concert's totally sold out," Jackie said, waving two tickets under Raven's nose. "Great seats. Front row center! Backstage passes, too."

"So, can you come?" Denise asked.

"You want to come?" Jackie urged.

"Are you coming?" pressed Curtis.

As her friends closed in, Raven wanted to tear her hair out. I cannot believe this is happening, she thought. Squeezing her eyes shut, she screamed, "Nooooo!" at the top of her lungs.

The shout echoed down the locker-lined hall. Raven opened her eyes to find everyone staring at her.

"I mean, no thanks," she added sheepishly.

Shaking his head, Eddie spoke up. "She has to spend *'quality time'* with her mom," he explained.

With a gasp, everyone stepped back, as if Raven were contagious.

"Eww," said Denise, bolting.

"That's too bad," said Jackie. She patted Raven's shoulder sympathetically before walking away.

"Yeah, too bad. Well, see ya," Curtis called as he hurried down the hall.

When everyone was gone, Raven turned to Eddie.

"So, what are *you* doing this weekend?" she asked glumly.

"Going to the movies with a friend," he

replied. "We're going to see *Ninja Vampires from Outer Space*. See, this vampire comes to Earth 'cause he sucked all the blood on his planet and—"

Eddie's lips kept moving, but his words suddenly faded away. Instead, Raven heard faint strains of harp music—the perfect accompaniment to the heavenly vision she saw walking toward her. And *this* vision had nothing to do with the future. This boy was most definitely a part of Raven's present.

He was the finest guy at Bayside—tall, dark, and handsome, with a killer smile and a confident stride. As he walked by Raven, he reached out and gave Eddie a tight homeboy handshake before moving on down the hall. Tuning back in, Raven suddenly realized her best friend *knew* this boy.

"—and garlic doesn't work on these dudes," Eddie continued, "'cause they're from outer space, and there's no garlic in outer space . . . that we know of."

"Wait a minute," Raven said, cutting him off. "You *know* that guy?"

Eddie looked over his shoulder. "Oh, you mean Ricky?" he asked. "That's who I'm going to the movies with."

Raven's jaw dropped. "I've been trying to get that guy to notice me all year!" she cried.

Suddenly Raven had an inspiration.

"Wait a minute, wait a minute. What about this?" she said. "I 'run into you' at the movies and act surprised, right? And you can be, like, 'What's up, Rae? This is my homie. Come join us.' And then I look into his big, brown, beautiful eyes and I'll say—Oh, I don't know what I'll say. I'll be too nervous!"

Raven paused. "But I'll look great," she added. "You know, 'cause that's a given."

"One problem," said Eddie. "How are you

going to get out of doing something with your mom?"

Suddenly, Raven felt the whole world freeze in time—

Through her eye
The vision runs
Flash of future
Here it comes—

I see my mother again.

She's got a tissue in her hand. She's lifting it to her nose and . . . she's blowing.

Ohmigosh! She's blowing! She's blowing her nose!

When Raven came out of her vision, she turned to Eddie. "I just had the best vision!" she cried.

"Did it involve me and Halle Berry?" Eddie asked.

Raven scowled. "No. I only see things that are actually *going* to happen," she told Eddie flatly. "And I just saw my mom blowing her nose. Which obviously means she's going to get a cold, which means my Saturday just opened up!"

Raven grinned. "No 'quality time'!" she exclaimed happily.

Eddie frowned at Raven.

Realizing how that sounded, she quickly added, "I just feel bad that she's going to get sick."

Eddie kept frowning. But Raven didn't care. Her worries were over, and her plan to meet the boy of her dreams was just beginning.

Ricky, baby, she thought, get ready to be dazzled!

Chapter Three

Saturday morning, Raven hovered in the kitchen, circling her mother like a nurse.

"Are you sure you're not feeling sick?" demanded Raven. She placed her palm on her mother's forehead, then touched her cheeks. "Not a tad bit stuffy? A little drippy?"

Mrs. Baxter waved her daughter away. But a moment later, Raven was back, thrusting a tissue under her mother's nose.

"Here," said Raven, "blow for me, Mother."

"Stop. Stop!" Mrs. Baxter cried.

"Blow. Blow!" Raven demanded.

Finally, to make her daughter happy, Mrs. Baxter blew into the tissue.

"Thank you," said Raven, tossing the

tissue away. "Are you sure you don't—"

"Nope," said Mrs. Baxter with a shake of her head. "Feelin' good. Ready for our big day today!"

She looked at Raven. "How about you?" Mrs. Baxter asked. "Are you all set for our big day today?"

Defeated, Raven felt she had no choice. Mission Boyfriend was in jeopardy. If her mother wasn't sick yet, then she'd have to switch to Plan B.

"Mom, hate to tell you this," Raven said with a frown. "But . . . ah, Mr. Petracelli just stuck me with this research assignment, which means I have to spend all day in the library."

Mrs. Baxter's face fell. "Oh well, honey, it's okay," she said with a sigh. "We'll have plenty of other times we can get together. Next Saturday at ten is good for me. How about you?"

Raven opened her mouth.

"Great, it's a date!" said Mrs. Baxter before Raven had the chance to weasel out of *another* Saturday. Grabbing her cup of tea, Raven's mother headed for the living room.

"Bye, Mom," said Raven, relieved.

Behind Raven, Cory had been silently watching his big sister's little show. He gave her a slimy smile of approval.

"The old library research trick," he said with a nod. "A classic."

"I don't know what you're talking about," Raven replied.

"Oh, I think you do," Cory said, raising an eyebrow.

"Oh, there's *thinking* going on in here?" called Raven's dad, who was just coming down the back stairs. "I must be in the wrong house."

Whoa! That was close—Cory almost blew

Part One

"And now the crowd can *stop* hugging,"
Eddie told Raven.

"So," Chelsea said, "what are you gonna do?"

"It's not like you had a vision of me failing the test," Eddie told Raven.

**"Eddie's playing for an ice-cold root beer,"
said Chelsea.**

"Wait!" Eddie said. "I thought I heard a *former* friend of mine."

"Man, you got my back on this one, Rae," Eddie said.

"Tell me there is *not* a bird on my head,"
said Raven.

"Hey, you want to play some one-on-one?"
Raven asked.

"Kids?" Mrs. Baxter called
from the living room.

"Listen," Mrs. Baxter said,
"what are you doing Saturday?"

"What about this?" Raven said. "I 'run into you' at the movies and act surprised."

"Here," said Raven, "blow for me, Mother."

"We're going to see *Farewell to Forever*,"
Mrs. Baxter said.

"Let me just re-butter your popcorn
for you," Raven said.

"This movie is so sad," Mrs. Baxter said.
"You want a tissue?"

"Until that time, farewell to forever,"
Raven and Mrs. Baxter mouthed along
with the movie.

my plan, Raven thought, watching her dad put on his apron to start breakfast. Time for a little payback, she decided.

"Actually, Dad," said Raven, grabbing Cory by the shoulders and holding him in place. "Cory was thinking that, ah, you two need to spend some more 'quality time' together. He was hoping for this afternoon."

Mr. Baxter grinned in surprise. "Really?" he said. "That would be great!"

Fake smile plastered across his chubby cheeks, Cory nodded. "That *would* be great," he said through clenched teeth.

"Yeah!" said Mr. Baxter as he grabbed the phone. "I'll just call one of the chefs to cover for me at the restaurant."

As Mr. Baxter punched in the numbers, Cory glared at his sister. Now it was Raven's turn to offer a slimy smile.

"Have a nice Saturday," she sang as she

ducked out of the kitchen and ran up the back stairs. She had some serious dazzle-making to do before she "accidentally" ran into Eddie and Ricky at the movies.

Later that afternoon, Raven had no trouble locating Ricky in the crowded movie theater. She just followed that heavenly harp music, and there he was, looking angelic in a worn denim jacket and a radiant smile.

And, oh, yeah. Eddie was there, too.

The two boys were sitting together at the far end of a row. They talked and ate popcorn as they waited for the movie to begin.

There's only one thing standing between me and Ricky now, thought Raven. Well, not really standing. *Sitting* would be more accurate. A half dozen moviegoers filled the seats between Raven and her potential boyfriend. But Raven wasn't about to let *them* stop her.

Just a few final checks, she thought, adjusting her bright red, hooded sweater jacket and the flower in her hair. Then, when she was sure her dazzle power was off the charts, Raven took a deep breath and made her move.

"Eddie?" Raven called across the row in mock surprise. "Edward? Oh my goodness, is that you?"

Eddie and Ricky both looked up.

Immediately, Raven barreled toward them, jostling the people in their seats.

"Oh, 'scuse me," said Raven as she scooted past. "That's my friend. 'Scuse me. Watch your tootsies. Comin' through."

Eddie glared at Raven. As far as he was concerned, this whole Mission Boyfriend plan was wack. But Raven didn't care what Eddie thought. Ignoring the look he gave her, she plopped down in the seat next to him. With a nervous smile, she met Ricky's eyes and patiently waited for Eddie to start the introduction they had rehearsed on the phone the night before. But Eddie just sat there like a lump.

C'mon, Eddie, get with the program, Raven thought, jamming her elbow into his ribs.

"And!" Eddie blurted out in pain. "*What* a coincidence it is to see you here at the movies . . . my unattached friend, Raven. . . ."

When Eddie stalled, Raven gave him another poke. Like a mechanical doll, he started up again.

"Whose phone number I happen to know," he droned, "if anyone should want it."

Ricky didn't seem to notice Eddie's sarcasm. He reached out politely to shake Raven's hand.

"Hi, I'm Ricky," he said with another radiant smile.

"And I'm Raven," she replied dreamily.

Chill, girl, Raven warned herself. Stay focused, and do *not* swoon.

Unfortunately, Raven failed to take her own advice. Temporarily lost in a love fog, she didn't notice Eddie's bucket of popcorn sitting between her and Ricky. As she reached out to shake hands, she accidentally knocked the bucket over—right onto Ricky's lap.

Raven gasped. "Oh, I'm so sorry!"

"It's okay," said Ricky, brushing the kernels to the floor.

But it wasn't okay with Eddie. "That was *my* popcorn!" he told Raven. "Extra large," he added meaningfully, "with butter."

"Eddie!" Raven cried.

"Scat!" barked Eddie, waving his hand toward the exit.

Frowning, Raven stood up. "I'll be right back," she told Ricky. Then Raven started to climb over the row of moviegoers again.

"Shake it off, Raven," she muttered as she maneuvered past the seats. "Shake it off.

Everything's okay." You messed up, girl, she told herself. But it can't get any worse. "I'm good. I'm good. Oh—"

Suddenly, Raven tripped over a man's long legs at the end of the row. She went sailing right into the aisle.

What did I say about it not getting any worse? she asked herself. She was lying face-down on the disgusting, sticky movie theater floor. Jumping to her feet, she glanced back down the row toward Ricky and Eddie. Unfortunately, they were looking right at her.

Okay, thought Raven, so they saw me fall. But at least Ricky seemed concerned about it.

"I'm good! I'm good!" she called, waving.

Eddie, she noted, didn't look so concerned. He was too busy laughing his face off.

With a huff, Raven pointed at the floor. "Watch that step. Maintenance! Hello!" she called. Then she beat it to the lobby.

Things couldn't possibly get any worse, she told herself again as she walked through the double doors. But just then she saw something that gave "worse" a whole new meaning: Mr. and Mrs. Baxter and her little brother, Cory, were all standing in line at the concession stand.

Raven's jaw dropped. Before she could hide, the doors to the theater behind her opened and a bloodcurdling scream echoed through the lobby. Everyone turned to look in her direction—including the Baxters.

"Hey, family," she squeaked cheerfully. But what she thought was, *I am so busted.*

Chapter Four

"**R**ae, what are you doing here?" Mr. Baxter asked in surprise.

"Yeah, big sister," Cory said smugly. "I thought you were at the *library*, doing *research*."

"Well, you know . . . I *was*, see, but," Raven stammered. "There's a really, *really* good explanation, for all of this, you know. . . ."

Cory crossed his arms. "We're waiting," he said.

"W-well," stuttered Raven. "Um . . ."

Suddenly Mrs. Baxter stepped forward and put her arms around Raven. "She must have finished early, gone home, and seen my note," she said.

"What note?" Mr. Baxter asked.

"Dad, the note," said Raven, seeing a way out of this mess. "Mama, you tell him."

"I left her a note so she'd know where we were and wouldn't worry," Mrs. Baxter explained.

"Exactly," said Raven, nodding enthusiastically. "And I know where you are, and I'm not worried. Whew!"

Mrs. Baxter took her daughter's arm. "Well, you guys better go ahead. Your movie is about to start."

Cory groaned. "Our movie is for babies."

"Honey," Mrs. Baxter said gently, "you're just not old enough to see other movies."

"Yeah," said Cory, "but why do I have to see *Quest of the Bunny People*?"

"*That's* what we're seeing?" Mr. Baxter asked. He was clearly disappointed. "Any ninjas in that?"

Cory sadly shook his head. Mr. Baxter frowned. As father and son trudged toward the theater, Mrs. Baxter turned to her daughter.

"I'm so glad you came," she said with a grin. "We're going to see *Farewell to Forever*."

But all Raven could think of were Ricky's big brown eyes. She couldn't let this chance slip away. "Mom, I—" she began.

Before Raven could continue, Mrs. Baxter took her by the hand and said, "It's a tragic tale about two lovers who are so close, yet so far away."

I can relate, thought Raven, looking longingly at the doors of the movie theater where she'd left Ricky and Eddie sitting.

Mrs. Baxter pulled Raven into another theater. The lights had dimmed, and *Farewell to Forever* was just starting to roll on the screen.

"These look good," whispered Mrs. Baxter,

pointing to two empty seats near the front row.

As they sat down, Raven suddenly shivered and pulled up the big hood of her sweater jacket.

"Oh, hey, Mom," she said, touching her mother's forehead. "Don't you think it's a bit drafty in here? That's not good for your cold, right? How's that coming?"

Mrs. Baxter waved her hand. "I told you, I'm fine," she insisted.

Then Mrs. Baxter pulled her enormous purse onto her lap. "Hey, are you hungry?" she whispered.

"Hungry?" said Raven. That gave her an idea. "Yes, Mama, I am. So I need to go to the candy counter, right? It could take a while. Long line. About an hour. See ya."

Raven jumped up, but her mother dragged her back down. "Honey, it's crazy to pay those prices," she said. Then she plunged her hands into her bottomless bag.

"Let's see," Mrs. Baxter said, sorting through piles of plastic sacks. "I've got popcorn, chips, sandwiches. . . . Do you want tuna or chicken?"

Shoot, thought Raven, glancing into her mother's purse. She's got a convenience store in there!

"You know," said Raven, "what *I* want, you couldn't have in that bag."

"Try me," Mrs. Baxter scoffed.

"Chocolate-covered raisins?" Raven guessed hopefully.

Mrs. Baxter immediately whipped out a huge bag full of chocolate-covered raisins and dangled it under her daughter's nose.

"$2.69 a pound," she bragged.

"Great." Raven sighed and took the bag.

Sorry, Mama, but we're onto Mission

Boyfriend Plan C now, Raven thought. This calls for *drastic* measures. When her mother turned away, Raven opened the bag of candy and "accidentally" spilled it onto the floor.

"Oh, Mom!" Raven cried, pointing to the mess. "I'm so sorry. Let me go get you some more."

Before her mother could protest, Raven was bookin' out of the theater! "Be right back. My treat!" she called as she hurried up the aisle.

Then, suddenly feeling that familiar tingling, Raven stopped beside a strange woman in another row. "You're not going to like that seat," Raven warned her.

The woman seemed confused by Raven's words—until the guy behind her propped his big, smelly, *bare* feet right on the back of her chair.

It's a doggone shame, thought Raven, continuing toward the exit. But sometimes my predictions stink!

Chapter Five

Raven burst through the theater doors, raced across the lobby, and ran face-first into the giant *Ninja Vampires from Outer Space* sign.

I'm a girl on a mission, so don't block my position! Raven said silently, knocking aside the cardboard ninja with a martial arts kick.

Inside the theater, the movie had already started. Up on the screen, space ninja vampires battled for control of the universe. Raven made her way down the aisle. Once again, she had to cross the row of annoyed moviegoers.

"Coming through. 'Scuse me. So sorry," Raven said over the complaints of the people in the seats. Finally, she plopped down next to Eddie.

But when Raven leaned forward to say *hey* to Ricky, his seat was empty.

"Hey, where's Ricky?" Raven whispered.

"He went to go get himself some popcorn," Eddie snapped when he saw Raven's *empty* hands. "He asked if I wanted some, but I said *no* because *Raven's* gonna be coming back with mine, so I'll just wait . . . and wait and *wait*!"

"Sorry," Raven said.

With a snort of disgust, Eddie slumped back into his seat to watch the movie. But Raven refused to shut up.

"See, I ran into my whole family in the lobby," she told him. "And now I'm stuck watching this lame movie with my mom. So, when Ricky gets back, I want you to tell him—"

"Tell me what?" asked Ricky as he sat down in his seat. He was holding a full bucket of popcorn.

Raven batted her eyelashes. "I want to tell you that I forgot the popcorn," she said sweetly.

"That's okay. We can share mine," he replied, offering the bucket to her.

Raven's heart melted. "We're *sharing*," she whispered to Eddie.

"Hello," Eddie whispered back. "Your mom's gonna bust you if you don't get your butt back there."

"I know," she said, her shoulders sagging. And thanks so much for the reality check, she thought.

But a second later, she sat straight up again. She'd just had a totally crazy idea! Raven shot Eddie a devious, Cory-worthy smile. When Eddie saw it, he shrank back in his seat—whatever was coming was far scarier than vampires or ninjas.

* * *

"This is so romantic!" Mrs. Baxter cried ten minutes later. She was now totally swept up in the "chick flick" playing in the theater next to the *Ninja Vampires from Outer Space*.

Reaching into her purse, Raven's mother took out a big red apple. After taking a sloppy bite, she waved the fruit under her daughter's nose.

"Want a bite?" she asked.

"Uh-uh," came the high-pitched reply from the person sitting next to Mrs. Baxter. It sounded a little like Raven—but it wasn't. It was Eddie, wearing Raven's big red sweater jacket with the hood pulled up.

Mrs. Baxter reached out to pat Raven's arm. "Honey, sounds like you're the one coming down with a cold," she said with concern.

"Uh-huh," Eddie replied again in a high-pitched voice.

"We'll stop and get you some throat

lozenges on the way home," said Mrs. Baxter, then she took Eddie's hand in hers and frowned. "And maybe some hand lotion, too," she added.

"What's taking Eddie so long?" Ricky asked in the next theater over.

"Who?" Raven said dreamily, staring at Ricky's handsome profile.

"Eddie," Ricky repeated.

"Right," Raven said, nodding. *"Who?"*

Ricky shook his head. "Never mind," he whispered. "Candy?"

Raven smiled and nodded. But when she looked at the box in Ricky's hand, she felt a tingling all over—

Through her eye
The vision runs
Flash of future
Here it comes—

I see my mother again.

Okay, what's she doing? She's leaning toward Eddie in my red sweater. She still thinks it's me. Thank goodness!

She's opening her mouth. She's asking him something—

"Rae," she whispers, "did you get my chocolate-covered raisins?"

Uh-oh, Eddie doesn't have them—which means I'm gonna get busted!

As Raven shook her head clear of her vision, she saw Ricky staring at her. He was still holding out his box of candy, waiting for her to take a piece.

"Are you all right?" he asked.

"Yes, I am," said Raven. Except I'm about to get busted, she thought. "Actually, no, I'm not, 'cause—"

Think fast, Raven, she told herself.

"Um . . . I don't like that candy," she added quickly. "I need to get my own." She jumped to her feet. "I'll be right back."

But the rest of the people in her row had finally had enough. With evil glares, they all threw their legs over the seats in front of them, blocking her exit.

Fine, thought Raven. I'll find another way out. Glancing down at the seats right in front of her, she saw a girl and boy kissing.

"Aw," Raven cooed. Then she reached down and yanked their heads apart. "'Scuse me!" she said as she stepped between them and over their seats.

"Sorry. Coming through!" she continued, as she jostled a whole *new* row of people. Too bad for them, she thought, but Plan C just isn't pretty.

* * *

On yet another screen in the cineplex, cute rabbits danced and sang and hugged a sad little bunny. Mr. Baxter's loud snore cut through the theater like a buzz saw. His head had lolled back, his eyes were closed, and his mouth was open. The beginnings of a second snore rumbled in his chest.

Cory elbowed his father. Mr. Baxter's eyes shot open. He sat up.

"If I have to watch this, so do you," Cory told his dad.

"Okay," said Mr. Baxter, rubbing his eyes. "What did I miss?"

Cory made a disgusted face. "Well, the Bunny People are sad, and Pitter Patter the Squirrel went out to get help in the Land of Happy Rainbows. But don't worry, there's still an hour and a half left!"

Chapter Six

Bursting through the theater doors, Raven raced to the concession stand.

"Oh, this line is way too long!" she groaned. The counter was so far away she needed a telescope to see it.

She looked around, trying to find a place to cut in. But the Alamo would have been easier to enter. These people were borderline hostile!

Walking past the parade of grumbling customers, Raven made her way up to the counter. Okay, what's the problem here? she wondered. I mean, hello? Handing out popcorn and candy cannot be that hard a job!

Spotting an employee's cap and apron hanging from a hook behind the concession stand, she got an idea. All she had to do was pretend to work at the concession stand for a minute, grab a box of chocolate-covered raisins, then make an excuse to leave with it.

Raven glanced around to make sure no one was looking. Then she quickly slipped behind the counter, smashed the cap down on her head, and tied the apron over her clothes. Taking a deep breath, she stepped up to the lone person working behind the counter.

"Hey, girl. Hey . . . *Becky*," said Raven, reading the employee's name badge. "I just started today. Let me help you out."

Becky nodded, looking extremely relieved. Raven smiled. She'd pulled it off! Then she turned to the folks waiting to be served.

"Hey, sir. What do you want?" she asked the next person in line. Before the man could answer, Raven blurted out, "Chocolate-covered raisins? Great choice! I like them, too."

Raven grabbed the box of candy and tried to make her getaway, but the counter girl stopped her.

"No, you stay," Becky commanded. "I'm going to go to the back and get some more containers. We're totally out."

Becky thrust a cardboard bucket into Raven's arms and pointed to a customer. "This guy wants popcorn," she said. "Extra butter, okay?"

"Okay. Thanks, Becky," said Raven. She dipped the bucket into the mound of popcorn behind the glass counter. Then she took the bucket to the butter dispenser and placed it under the spout. As Raven pumped the dispenser's handle, she looked nervously at the impatient customer.

"All right, Becky's going on a little break," she called over her shoulder, "so I'm going to get you some popcorn, sir."

But the dispenser wasn't cooperating. Only a few tiny droplets came out of the pump.

Raven pumped the handle again, this time harder. C'mon you stupid pump! she thought. She wanted nothing more than to get back to *Farewell to Forever* before her mother discovered Eddie was sitting next to her!

"Oh, there you go," Raven coaxed, continuing to pump the handle. "Go popcorn butter—come on!"

Finally, Raven banged the machine with her hand. Immediately, an ocean of greasy yellow topping gushed out of the spout.

"There you go, butter," said Raven, relieved. Like I figured, she said to herself—not that hard a job. I mean, *puh-lease*!

But when she turned to give the customer his popcorn, Raven noticed that the topping kept on streaming out of the dispenser. She hit the STOP button once. Twice. Three times.

"Whoa! Stop! Stop!" Raven commanded. But the flow didn't stop.

Raven grabbed a stack of napkins and held them against the spout in a futile effort to stem the buttery tide. Still the stream continued, threatening to drown Raven in a sea of oily yellow flavoring!

Grabbing a stack of paper cups, she placed them, one by one, under the spout to catch the runaway stream. All the while, Raven tried to play the crowd.

"How's everyone doing?" Raven asked. "I'm doing fine. Just great. Thanks for your patience!"

But by this time, the customers had totally run out of patience.

"Where's my soda?" barked the man who'd ordered the popcorn.

"How about those nachos?" snapped the woman behind him.

"I asked for licorice," a little girl whined. And the complaints kept coming—

"I want two boxes of bonbons."

"Can I get an extra straw?"

"Hurry up!"

"Okay! All right! Hang on!" cried Raven, still trying to stop the yellow river with her pathetic stack of paper cups. "Okay, who wanted licorice?"

A woman raised her hand and Raven hurled the box at her.

Then Raven grabbed another box. "Yo! Bonbons!" she called. "Heads up!"

Raven tossed the box to the crowd. "Honor system, people. Leave your money on the counter!"

Finally out of cups, Raven searched for something bigger to hold the streaming topping. Desperate, she took the cap off her head and placed it under the spout.

"Nachos! Where are my nachos?" demanded an irate customer.

"Nachos!" yelled another. "I want nachos, too. Don't forget *my* nachos."

"Okay, okay!" Raven shouted. But she couldn't find any nacho containers. That's when she remembered Becky had gone to get them.

Frantic, Raven grabbed a handful of nacho chips and held them under the flow of butter. When they were dripping with topping, Raven thrust the soggy mess into a customer's hands. The man made a face.

"It's the same as the cheese, only yellower," Raven insisted.

When she turned around to get more nachos, she slid across the greasy floor. "Whoa!" she cried as her feet slipped out from under her. *Splat!* She landed in a slimy puddle of topping.

When she rose, she saw that her cap had completely filled with popcorn topping and the butter was now overflowing onto the counter and floor!

At her wit's end, Raven yanked off her stacked black boot and looked at it regretfully. "I'm so sorry. I love you," she said, kissing her favorite footwear.

Whimpering, Raven thrust the tall boot under the flowing spout, at last controlling the overflow. "Look at that right there, that's brains," said Raven proudly.

Just then, Becky returned with the empty nacho containers. She took one look at the mess Raven had made, marched over to the butter dispenser, and yanked out the plug. The river of yellow halted instantly.

Oooooh, thought Raven. Why didn't I think of that? Trying to cover, she turned to the angry customers and held up her ruined footwear.

"Okay," called Raven. "Who ordered the boot with butter?"

Becky crossed her arms and glared furiously at Raven.

Frowning, Raven took off her apron. "It has been nice working with you, Becky," she said. Then she tucked the chocolate-covered raisins into her pocket and handed Becky two dollars to pay for them.

Only one thing left to do, thought Raven—get rid of this topping in my boot.

"Let me just re-butter your popcorn for ya," she said. *And* help you get rid of some of these annoying customers, she added silently. Then she poured the entire greasy contents of her boot onto the freshly popped popcorn.

With groans of "gross" and "disgusting" echoing in her ears, Raven hurried back to her mother's side, candy in hand.

Chapter Seven

Just as Raven left the lobby, her father entered it with Cory in tow.

With an hour left to go, Mr. Baxter had totally lost patience with *Quest of the Bunny People*. "Okay," the big man announced in a stern voice. "Clouds are *not* made out of cotton candy, bunnies do not talk, and trees don't hug you when you're sad. Those are lies we should not be teaching our children."

Mr. Baxter turned to Cory. "You think your mom will buy that?" he asked.

"No," said Cory.

Mr. Baxter thumped his chest. "A *real* ninja wouldn't care. We're going in," he declared, pointing to the theater showing *Ninja*

Vampires from Outer Space. Cory nodded, and the two of them rushed toward the doors.

As they burst into the theater, Mr. Baxter looked up at the screen. He stopped short, his eyes widening. "Ew," he said, "his brains are oozing out through his eye sockets."

Then a huge grin split Mr. Baxter's face. He grabbed Cory's hand. "Let's get a seat up close!" he exclaimed.

Meanwhile, in *Farewell to Forever*, Eddie, still wearing Raven's big hooded sweater jacket, was slumped down in his seat. He wished he was watching the ninja vampires movie.

"Dearest, I love you so much," said the actor on screen, as gloomy violin music played in the background.

At Eddie's side, Mrs. Baxter sobbed loudly and blew her nose in a wad of tissues.

"Pssst!" someone hissed from the aisle.

Eddie turned to find Raven hopping around on one foot, trying to stick the other one back into her boot.

Leaping up, Eddie quietly raced to Raven's side.

"Give these to my mom," said Raven, thrusting the chocolate-covered raisins into his hand.

But Eddie had had enough tragic violins and sobbing women to last him the rest of his life.

"*Your* candy, *your* mom, *your* jacket," he told her, trying to unzip the sweater jacket. "I'm going back to my movie."

No! Raven wailed silently. I want to get back to Ricky. I *need* to get back to Ricky. "Please, Eddie—" she begged.

But Eddie just shook his head and kept trying to unzip the jacket. "It's stuck," he moaned.

Raven and Eddie struggled with it, but the zipper refused to budge.

"Rae?" Mrs. Baxter said suddenly from her seat. "Did you get my chocolate-covered raisins?"

Eddie and Raven froze.

In a panic, Raven slipped her head under the big sweater and climbed inside—with Eddie still in it!

Her head peeked out from inside the hood. But her arms were trapped at her sides—because Eddie's arms still occupied the sleeves.

"Yes, Mom, coming," Raven called softly.

The two-headed, Eddie-and-Raven sweater-monster made its way back into the seat beside Mrs. Baxter. When they sat down, Eddie was squashed underneath Raven. Only his arms were free.

"You can have your raisins, Mom. I'll give

them to you right now," said Raven, hoping Eddie had heard her.

Eddie, clutching the candy in his left hand, waved the box helplessly. But Mrs. Baxter was sitting on their right!

"Not *left* now," prompted Raven, "*right* now."

Eddie quickly shifted the candy to his right hand and offered it to Mrs. Baxter.

"There you go, Mommy," said Raven as Mrs. Baxter took the box.

"Thank you," said Mrs. Baxter, still focused on the movie.

"But, dearest," cooed the actor on the screen, "you and little Rodney are all I have. . . ."

Mrs. Baxter sighed and dabbed her nose with yet another wad of tissues. "This movie is so sad," she sniffed. "I love it. You want a tissue?"

Mrs. Baxter passed Raven the box. "No,

thanks," Raven replied, even as Eddie grabbed a handful.

"Okay, maybe I will. I'll just use it to wipe my nose," said Raven, covering.

Wiping blindly, Eddie fumbled to find Raven's nose.

"Not my *ear*," complained Raven. "There, *there's* my nose."

With the tissue in Eddie's hand threatening to smother her, Raven blew her nose loudly. "Right, oh yeah, that was good," said Raven. "That's good, thank you."

But Eddie's hand just kept rubbing Raven's nose.

"Now I'm just gonna *stop*," said Raven. "I'm gonna stop. I'm gonna stop *now*!"

Finally, Eddie got the message. The soggy tissue hung loosely in his grip.

"Eww, that's nasty!" cried Raven. "Let me just *flick it* right over there."

Eddie dropped the tissue, then poked Raven impatiently and pointed in the direction of the lobby.

"Um, hey, Mom, you got something to drink?" Raven asked.

"Sure," Mrs. Baxter replied, reaching into her bag. She quickly produced two huge plastic bottles. "You want water or lemonade?" she asked.

Dang, thought Raven, looking at the giant bottles, that bag *is* bottomless.

"Surprise me," she told her mother. And, as Mrs. Baxter opened a bottle, Raven and Eddie scurried out of their seat and up the aisle.

A moment later, Mrs. Baxter turned to find Raven's seat empty.

Puzzled, Mrs. Baxter shrugged and went back to watching the movie.

Chapter Eight

In the lobby, Raven quickly slipped out of the big sweater and fanned herself.

"Okay," she told Eddie. "I don't think she saw us. So, when you go back in there, I want you to just sit down, be quiet—"

But Eddie yanked off the sweater and thrust it into Raven's arms.

"I *told* you, I'm not doing it anymore," he said.

"Eddie, come on," Raven pleaded. "I just want to go in there, say good-bye to Ricky, and then I'll be right back."

But Eddie just kept shaking his head.

"Look," Raven continued, "my mom is so into the movie, it doesn't matter who's sitting next to her. I'm telling you—"

"Oh yeah?" Eddie barked, cutting her off. "Is that why she leaned over *three* times to let you know how glad she was you were there?"

Raven's eyes widened. "She said that?"

"Yes," said Eddie, nodding.

Raven stared at him, speechless.

"And if you were sitting with her," he told Raven, "you would've heard it." Eddie turned his back on Raven and stalked away. But before he entered the theater, he turned back. "By the way, your mom's buying me panty hose on Thursday," he said. Then, with a slightly bewildered look on his face, he disappeared through the door.

Still stunned, Raven went back into the theater she'd just left and sat down next to her mother. "Sorry, Mom. Bathroom break," she whispered.

Mrs. Baxter smiled as Raven leaned on her

mother's shoulder and snuggled close, finally taking some *real* quality time.

But, just as Raven settled in, the screen went black and the lights came up.

"Wait," Raven said, confused. "Wait a minute. What's going on?"

Mrs. Baxter smiled and patted Raven's arm. "Honey, the movie is over," she told her.

Raven's heart sank. She'd missed the whole movie. Worse than that, she'd missed the time she could have spent with her mom.

"No!" cried Raven. "I mean—" She paused and sighed. "I don't want it to be over," she said.

"Me neither, honey," said Mrs. Baxter, putting an arm around Raven's shoulders. "But there's going to be other movies, other Saturdays."

Still frowning, Raven said, "I was just getting into this one."

Mrs. Baxter fought back a tear as she held her daughter close. Then she reached into her tissue box and blew her nose again. Raven's mind raced back to the vision she'd had at school the day before. "Mom!" Raven said, as the truth finally dawned on her. "You blew your nose like in my vision. But you're not doing it because you have a cold. You're doing it because you're crying at the movie."

Mrs. Baxter smiled and wiped her eyes. "It's the movie, and it's you, and it's me. And it's our time together," she said.

"Right, our time," murmured Raven.

"Honey, I love you," said her mother.

Raven nodded as she sadly realized that it was her own fault their time was up so soon.

After gathering her things, Mrs. Baxter led Raven up the aisle and back into the lobby.

"Wasn't this fun?" said Mrs. Baxter, squeezing

her daughter's hand. Then she paused, stroked Raven's skin, and asked, "Honey, what happened to your hands? They were so rough. What did you put on them?"

"Uh . . . *butter*," said Raven, catching a glimpse of the concession stand. And that was no lie, she thought.

Just then, Raven's father and brother emerged from the *Ninja Vampires* movie.

Mrs. Baxter folded her arms across her chest and frowned. Not only had her husband and son come out the *wrong* doors, they were now giving each other fake kung fu strikes.

"Baby, look, I know what you're thinking," said Mr. Baxter when he saw his wife's scowl. "We tried to make it through *The Bunny People*. But clouds are not made out of cotton candy, and—"

"Bunnies do not suck other bunnies' blood," pointed out Mrs. Baxter.

"Exactly!" cried Cory. "That'd be so cool."

Mr. Baxter nodded. "Those little sharp teeth in their furry little necks," he said, getting into it.

"Yeah!" exclaimed father and son together.

But Mrs. Baxter was still frowning. Shaking his head, Mr. Baxter sighed. They were busted and he knew it.

"We'll be outside," he told his wife sheepishly.

Just then, Eddie and Ricky walked out of the *Ninja Vampires* theater, too.

"Raven! Mrs. Baxter!" cried Eddie in fake astonishment. "What a lovely surprise it is to see you here today. I'm here with my friend Ricky, and we're going to grab a bite to eat."

Ricky smiled at Raven. "Want to come?" he asked.

Raven's heart skipped a beat. Obviously, Eddie had let him know what was up with her "quality time" Olympics. And he didn't seem to care. He actually *wanted* her to come!

"Honey, you should go," said Mrs. Baxter. Eyeing Ricky, she pulled Raven close and girlishly whispered, "He's fine!"

Raven smiled. "Okay," she said.

But as she started to leave with the two boys, she noticed her mother pause by a trash can and open her purse. Out came the mound of wet tissues her mom had used during the tearjerker. Suddenly, Raven was sorry all over again that she'd missed seeing the movie with her mother.

"You know what, Ricky?" she said, stopping before they left the lobby. "I think I'm going to hang out with my mom."

"Oh, okay," said Ricky with a shrug. "Then I guess I'll see you at school."

"Okay," said Raven. She was about to turn away when Eddie touched her shoulder.

"Yo, Rae," he said. "Good for you." Then he smiled and waved good-bye.

Seeing Raven wave to her friends, Mrs. Baxter walked up to her with a puzzled expression. "Honey, you didn't have to do that," she said.

"I know," said Raven, "but I really wanted to see the movie with you . . . again."

"Really?" said Mrs. Baxter. "But we just saw it."

"Yeah, well, I guess I just needed some more 'quality time,'" Raven said with a smile.

An hour and a half later, Raven and Mrs. Baxter were happily snuggled up together, totally engrossed in the tearjerker.

On screen, the gloomy violin melody played as the actor spoke his tragic lines: "Someday we'll be together again. Until that time . . . farewell to forever."

Their chins quivering, Raven and Mrs. Baxter mouthed the words along with the movie. Then mother and daughter burst into tears.

Sitting beside them, father and son looked completely lost—and completely miserable.

Finally, Mr. Baxter shook his head. Leaning over, he whispered to Cory, "I just wish somebody would get beaten up in this thing."

Gaze into the future and take a sneak peek at the next *That's So Raven* story. . . .

Adapted by Alice Alfonsi
Based on the series created by
Michael Poryes
Susan Sherman
Based on the teleplay written
by Susan Sherman

"**O**kay," said Raven Baxter, worriedly checking her watch, "she's almost here."

Raven plunged her hands into the shopping bag sitting on the coffee table and pulled out two pairs of brand-new shoes. "These or these?" Raven asked her best friend, Chelsea Daniels, who was sitting on the couch.

Chelsea studied the red stacked sandals and fringed suede boots. Both looked totally hot. But Chelsea knew no pair of shoes was going to solve Raven's *real* problem.

"Rae," said Chelsea in a firm voice, "you always freak out every time your cousin Andrea comes in from Europe."

And do you know *why*? Raven wanted to ask her. Because the girl is untouchable! She has perfect skin, perfect hair, perfect teeth. And she buys her clothes in places like France and Italy. How can I compete with that?

But Raven wasn't about to admit any of that—not to Chelsea, not to anyone.

"Girl, I am *fine*," Raven lied with a wave of her hand. An instant later, that same hand dove back into the shopping bag and pulled out two new hats. "I just need to know which hat says, 'Thanks for coming, but you need to go back to Paris.'"

"Rae," Chelsea said with a sigh, "she's only going to be here for a little while."

"Okay, I understand that," said Raven, putting down the hats and frantically fishing around inside the bag once more. "But does this *belt* say, 'Just because we're relatives, doesn't mean I have to like you'?"

Chelsea just shook her head.

Suddenly, the front door swung open and Eddie Thomas, Raven's other best friend, rushed in. "Okay, where's Andrea?" he asked with an eager grin. "Is my little French pastry here yet?"

Raven scowled. One whiff of Parisian perfume and my boy turns into a double-crossing dog, she thought. No, make that a French poodle.

"Eddie, how can you like her so much?" Raven snapped. "She is such a snob."

"Because she's not like other girls around

here, Rae," Eddie replied. "She's lived in Rome, London, Paris. . . . And she's turned me down in four different languages: *nein, nyet, non*, and the ever-popular 'ain't gonna happen.'"

"You know what?" said Raven, buckling her brand-new red belt around her new low riders. "She is so phony. I can't stand that about her."

Just then, Raven's parents and her little brother, Cory, waddled through the front door, weighed down with enough designer luggage to crush a small car.

Waltzing in behind them, swinging her expensive matching handbag, was Raven's cousin, Andrea.

"Look who's here!" cried Mr. Baxter, his back bent from the weight of the girl's suit-cases.

"Ravey!" exclaimed Andrea, rushing across the living room with a squeal of delight.

What a fake, Raven thought. Then, with a

fake squeal of her own, she gushed, "Oh, hi, Andrea! My girl, what is goin' on?"

The two girls met in the middle of the living room. "Smooches!" cried Raven, and they gave each other phony air kisses.

Raven gave her cousin a quick once-over and was sorry to see that her wardrobe looked as chic as ever. Andrea's shiny copper pants and matching top perfectly complemented her fur-lined leather coat. And her straightened hair looked sleek and glossy beneath a trendy, brimless cap. From her perfect shoes to her flawless makeup, Andrea always looked like she'd just stepped off a fashion show runway.

Unfortunately, her supermodel look came with an attitude to match. "It's *Ahn-drea* now," Raven's cousin announced in a snobbish tone.

"Oh," said Raven, though what she wanted to say was *Oh, puh-lease!*

"I changed it when we moved to Paris,"

Andrea continued. "We live right near the Eiffel Tower." She paused to take off her tinted glasses and look down her nose at Raven. "That's the tall, pointy thing you might've seen in magazines."

Raven forced a laugh—mostly to keep herself from forcing those trendy glasses down her stuck-up cousin's throat.

"Ooh, girl," Raven replied, "how I will miss that sense of humor when you go back. . . . *When* is that exactly?"

"In a week," said Raven's father, rushing in to defuse the potentially lethal glares the cousins were giving each other. "But until then we're going to have a *nice* family visit. Unlike the *last* one—" he added, throwing a pointed look at Raven—"when the gum was put in the hair—"

"—after the doll was put in the toilet," added Raven's mother, throwing an equally pointed look at Andrea.

At once, both girls cried, "She started it!" Then they both burst into fake laughter. Raven's mother and father just rolled their eyes. This was going to be one long week—and everybody knew it.

"So, um, Andrea," said Raven, after Mr. and Mrs. Baxter had gone upstairs. "You remember Eddie and Chelsea."

Andrea aimed her plastic smile across the room and said, "So, Chelsea, Cory tells me you two are dating."

"What?" Chelsea cried, outraged. She glared down at Raven's plump younger brother.

"We gotta share our love, baby," said Cory. Then he pursed his lips and gave Chelsea his *call-me-Doctor-Love* look.

Chelsea fumed. Get real, she was about to tell him, you're a little kid, and you wear bunny pajamas. But Cory fled for the stairs before Chelsea could get the words out.

"Well," Andrea said, turning toward the stairs herself, "I'm going to go freshen up now. You know how tiring those long international flights can be." Pausing, she glanced back at Raven and added, "Oh, right. You don't. See you, Ravey."

"Oh, see you soon," Raven called sweetly. But as soon as her cousin disappeared, she turned to her friends. "'I'll see you, Ravey,'" she said, mimicking Andrea's stuck-up voice. Raven squeezed her eyes shut. "Oh, she gets on my nerves!" she cried in frustration. "Everything is so perfect with her. Perfect life, perfect hair, perfect shoes. And then she comes into my life, interrupts everything, and you know—"

Suddenly, Raven's head started to spin. She felt her skin begin to tingle and the world seemed to freeze in time—

Through her eye
The vision runs
Flash of future
Here it comes—

I see my kitchen at night . . . which night? I don't know, but my super-snobby cousin is standing by the kitchen table. As usual, she's totally stylin' in an all-white designer outfit with a matching beret on top of her sleek black hair.

Eddie's there too, standing right in front of her. He's all puppy-eyed and practically drooling, the traitorous dog.

Yo, wait a minute . . . what's my cousin doing? She's leaning toward Eddie, taking his chin in her hand, puckering her lips, and—

No!

I am NOT seeing this! She did not—

"*Kiss* Eddie?" Raven blurted out as she shook free of her vision. Shocked, she turned to her two best friends. Chelsea looked horrified. And Eddie . . .

Raven frowned. Eddie looked like he'd just won a trip to Paris.

Get Cheetah Power!

the Cheetah Girls

Includes An Alternate Ending & Exclusive Behind-The-Scenes Look

Now on DVD and Video

Groove to the sound of all your favorite shows

Disney Channel Soundtrack Series

Disney's
Kim Possible
TV Soundtrack

The Cheetah Girls
TV Soundtrack

Lizzie McGuire
TV Soundtrack

Pixel Perfect
Soundtrack

Also, look for...

- *The Proud Family* TV Series Soundtrack
- *That's So Raven* TV Series Soundtrack

Collect them all!